Flavia
THE ROMANCE OF LIFE

for
Applause, Inc.

Printed in Italy by Malipiero S.p.A. Editore

To receive the "Romance of Life Quarterly" publication
or to join The Flavia Club write:
Flavia Club, Dept. 9
925 De La Vina, Third Floor
Santa Barbara, California
93101 USA
Telephone: 805-564-6909

© Flavia Weedn
All Rights Reserved under international
and Pan American copyright convention

Designed by James O. Frazier

ISBN 0-929632-10-9 Library Of Congress No. 90-81074

Flavia AND THE VELVETEEN RABBIT

ORIGINAL STORY BY MARGERY WILLIAMS

RETOLD BY FLAVIA & LISA WEEDN
ILLUSTRATED BY FLAVIA WEEDN

Once
you believe
in wonder,
it stays with you
always.

Especially for Sydney Rose...and for all of us who know the magic called real.

There was once a Velveteen Rabbit, and in the beginning he was very beautiful. He was soft and bunchy, as a rabbit should be, and his coat was winter white. He had real thread whiskers, his eyes were a lavender blue…and his nose was pink like the lining of his ears.

It was Christmas morning, and while the little Rabbit sat very still inside a bright colored stocking, he was very excited as he looked all around the room. Sights and smells of the season filled the air; there was a tree with cookie dough ornaments and twinkling stars and branches of holly and of mistletoe…there were apples and oranges and cinnamon sticks…handmade toys and gifts…and most of all, a feeling of love.

The little Rabbit knew he must be a part of it all when he saw the ribbon around his neck with a tag that read ''For Flavia''.

For a while, in the morning after Flavia had unwrapped him, she held him and played with him, and then aunts and uncles and cousins had come…other gifts had been opened…and in the excitement of Christmas dinner and all the celebration…the Velveteen Rabbit became covered over with paper and ribbons and was forgotten.

For a long time he lived with the other toys in the toy box in the corner, and no one thought very much about him. He was naturally shy, and since he was made only of velveteen, many of the other toys teased him. Some, like the model train, acted like they were better than he was, and always bragged that they were real.

Flavia's toy cat, who looked just like a real cat, thought he was special because he was the most beautiful, with his long fur and soft pink nose. Flavia's bear thought he was the best because he had fancier clothes than the other toys and his paws looked just like a real bear's paws.

The Rabbit could not pretend he looked like a real rabbit, for he didn't know that they even existed. He knew he was filled with string and sawdust and that important and modern toys were not made of anything like that anymore, so he never talked about it with the other toys. He kept his feelings inside because he thought the other toys would laugh at him.

The elephant kept going on about how he was surely the best because he was the strongest, the biggest and the bravest…while the long-necked giraffe argued he was the most important because he was the tallest and could see more. The poor little Rabbit, because he was different and couldn't do some of the things the other toys could do, thought he was not as good as they were…and so he felt very lonely inside. Listening to the other toys made him feel sad and unimportant, and he realized the only person who was kind to him at all was the Skin Horse.

The Skin Horse had lived there longer than any of the others. He was so old that his coat was bald in patches and showed the seams underneath, and most of the hairs in his tail had been pulled out and used to make bead necklaces for Flavia and her friends.

He was wise for he had seen many toys come into the house only to stay on the shelf and never be played with...and he knew they were only toys...and would never turn into anything else.

The Rabbit didn't know what the Skin Horse knew...that being a model of something or pretending to be something you are not, is not being Real.

Being Real comes from something inside...and being the most beautiful, the bravest or the tallest has nothing to do with what makes you special or important.

Childhood magic, you see, is very strange and wonderful, and doesn't have to be explained to those playthings that are old and wise and experienced like the Skin Horse, for they understand all about it.

hat is Real?" asked the Rabbit one day while they were talking. "Does it mean having a stick-out handle, and things that buzz inside you?"

"Real isn't how you are made," said the Skin Horse. "It's a thing that happens to you. When a child loves you for a long, long time, not just to play with, but REALLY loves you, then you become Real."

"Does it hurt?" asked the Rabbit.

"Sometimes," said the Skin Horse, for he was always truthful. "When you are Real, you don't mind being hurt."

"Does it happen all at once, like being wound up," he asked, "or bit by bit?"

"It doesn't happen all at once," said the Skin Horse. "You become. It takes a long time. That's why it doesn't often happen to people who break easily, or have sharp edges, or who have to be carefully kept. Generally, by the time you are Real, most of your hair has been loved off, and your eyes drop out and you get loose in the joints and very shabby. But these things don't matter at all, because once you are Real you can't be ugly, except to people who don't understand."

"I suppose *you* are Real?" said the Rabbit. And then he wished he had not said it, because he thought he might have hurt the Skin Horse's feelings, but the Skin Horse only smiled.

"Jack, Flavia's uncle, made me Real," he said. "That was many years ago; but once you are Real you can't become unreal again. It lasts for always."

The Rabbit sighed. He thought it would be a long time before this magic called Real happened to him. He longed to become Real, to know what it felt like; but it made him feel sad to think he would fade and grow wrinkled and shabby and lose his eyes and whiskers. He wished he could become it without these things happening to him.

ometimes when Flavia's grandma, whom they called Mammo, would clean the house, she would gather up the toys in her apron and toss them back into the toy box. Most of the toys hated it because they hurt when they fell. Sometimes they even broke, and had to be given to the Hankyman, the fix-it man who came by Flavia's house every Tuesday; but the Rabbit didn't mind too much when Mammo threw him into the toy box, for wherever he was thrown he came down soft.

One night, when Flavia was going to bed, she couldn't find the rag doll that always slept with her . . . so, as she passed by the toy box, she saw the Velveteen Rabbit, pulled him up by the ear, and carried him to bed.

That night, and for many nights after, the Rabbit slept in Flavia's bed. At first he found it very uncomfortable, for Flavia hugged him very tightly, and sometimes she rolled over on him, or pushed him so far under the pillow that the Rabbit could barely breathe. And...he missed those long moonlight hours in the toy box when all the house was quiet...and when he talked with the Skin Horse.

Very soon, though, the Rabbit grew to like it, for Flavia would talk to him and she would make tunnels for him under the covers...tunnels that she said were like the places that real rabbits lived in.

Always after Flavia got in bed, Mama would tell her a story, kiss her goodnight and leave the door open just a little. And, before she would fall asleep, Flavia and the Velveteen Rabbit would share feelings they kept in their hearts. Flavia would whisper how at night she would make secret wishes and tell them to the moon… and how she thought Jack, her uncle, was magic.

And the Rabbit would lie close to her and listen, and would think about how much he wished he was real.

Flavia would let the Rabbit snuggle down under the covers beside her, and she would sleep with her arm wrapped close around him all night long.

During the rest of the Wintertime, they would play in the snow and, as time went on, the little Rabbit was very happy . . . so happy that he never noticed how his beautiful velveteen fur was getting shabbier and shabbier, or how his tail was coming unsewn, and all the pink was rubbing off his nose where Flavia had kissed him. He didn't even notice that the ribbon he had worn at Christmas time was gone.

Spring came and they had long days playing in the funny old chairs on the porch, in the yard under the fig tree, or sitting in a big arm chair reading stories.

Flavia and her brother, Willie, would dress the little Rabbit up in clothes that Mama would make, and give him rides in the wagon...and everywhere they went, the Rabbit went, too.

Sometimes they would pretend some of the flowers were fairies...and they would make fairy huts in the flower beds, or at the trunk of the fig tree or beside the back porch steps.

One of their favorite things was to pull the wagon through the field of tall grass behind the house and climb to the top of the hill. They would sit there together and talk and sing and tell stories while they looked down at the house and the wild flowers below.

And once, on a Sunday late afternoon when Flavia was called by Jack and Willie to put on a show...the Rabbit was left on the grass 'til after dark, and Jack had to come and look for him because Flavia couldn't go to sleep without him.

He was wet through and through and dirty from being on the ground by the tree trunk, so Mammo had to rub off the dirt with a corner of her apron.

When the Rabbit was safe and warm on the pillow beside her, Flavia heard Mammo say, "All that love for just a toy Bunny!" Flavia sat up in bed and put her arm around him quickly. "But, Mammo, don't say that! He isn't a toy! He isn't! He's REAL!"

When the little Rabbit heard that he was very happy. And, while Flavia was tying one of her ribbons around his neck, he thought about what the Skin Horse had told him and knew it was true at last...the childhood magic had happened to him, and he was a toy no longer. He was REAL. Flavia herself had said it!

That night he was almost too happy to sleep, and so much love stirred in his little sawdust heart that he thought it would burst. And into his eyes...that had long lost their shine...there came a look of wisdom and beauty...the kind that comes when you know a secret. The little Rabbit wondered if, when tomorrow came, Willie and Jack would know what had happened...and if they would notice the ribbon...and see how happy he was.

That was a wonderful Summer! Flavia and the Velveteen Rabbit were becoming close friends. Sometimes she would take him with her when she climbed the fig tree, for this was her favorite place to dream, or sometimes they would just sit in the funny old chairs and talk about things.

One day, she saw Jack tie a colored string around the neck of the Skin Horse and she overheard him say, "I love you, and always want you to remember that you are as beautiful to me now as the first time I saw you long ago." And of course, to Jack, the Skin Horse really was beautiful.

Flavia looked at the Velveteen Rabbit and wondered if he knew just how much she loved him. During the rest of that summer she would remember Jack's words to the Skin Horse . . . and she would whisper into the little Rabbit's ear every time she tied a bright new ribbon around his neck, "I love you, little Rabbit," hoping that somehow deep inside he'd understand.

In the long June evenings, she and Willie would tell stories to the Rabbit or play hide and seek with him on the porch or in the shadows. They would play games with the ribbons, and sometimes Flavia would make him a little nest in the tall grass where he would be cozy and warm, for she was a kind-hearted little girl and loved the little Rabbit so.

Once while the Rabbit was there alone in the field where Flavia had put him and he was watching the ants go to and from their hole in the ground...he suddenly saw two strange animals creep out of the tall grass near him.

They were rabbits like himself, but a different color and more furry, and they looked brand new. They must have been very well made, for their seams didn't show at all, and they changed shape in a strange way when they moved; one minute they were long and thin and the next minute fat and bunchy, instead of always looking the same like he did.

Their feet were soft on the ground, and they crept quite close to him, twitching their noses…while the little Rabbit stared hard, trying to see the stick-out-handle. He knew that things that jump usually have a handle with which to wind them up, or a key, or a button to push…or a place for batteries.

But he couldn't see anything like that…so he thought they must be some new kind of toy rabbit he'd never seen before.

They stared at him, and the little Rabbit stared back. And all the time their noses twitched.

"Why don't you get up and play with us?" one of them asked.

"I don't feel like it," said the Rabbit. He didn't want to explain that he couldn't because he had no handle or battery.

"But," said the furry rabbit, "it's as easy as anything." And he gave a big hop sideways and stood on his hind legs. "I don't believe you can!" he said.

"I can!" said the little Rabbit. "I can jump higher than anything!" He meant when Flavia threw him…but of course he didn't want to say so.

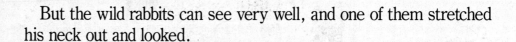

"Can you hop on your hind legs?" asked the furry rabbit. That was a terrible question, for the Velveteen Rabbit had no hind legs at all! The back of him was made all in one piece, and except for his tail, he was like a pincushion. He sat still in the grass, and hoped that the other rabbits wouldn't notice.

"I don't want to!" he said again.

But the wild rabbits can see very well, and one of them stretched his neck out and looked.

"He hasn't got any hind legs at all!" he called out. "Imagine that! A rabbit without any hind legs!" And they began to laugh.

"I have!" cried the little Rabbit. "I have got hind legs! I am just sitting on them!"

"Then stretch them out and show me, like this!" said the wild rabbit. And he began to whirl 'round and dance, 'til the little Rabbit got very dizzy just watching.

"I don't like dancing," the Velveteen Rabbit said. "I'd rather sit still!"

He knew when he said it that this was not true. He wanted to dance and had often watched Flavia, Willie and Jack put on shows for the family on Sundays and he always wished he could dance with them. Suddenly a funny new tickly feeling ran through him, and he felt he would give anything in the world to be able to jump high and dance like these rabbits did.

The strange rabbit stopped dancing, and came very close. He came so close this time that his long whiskers brushed against the Velveteen Rabbit's ear, and then he wrinkled his nose suddenly, flattened his ears and jumped backwards.

"He doesn't smell like a rabbit!" he said. "He isn't a rabbit at all! He isn't real!"

"I AM Real!" said the little Rabbit. "I am Real! Flavia said so!" And he almost began to cry.

Just then there was a sound of footsteps, and Flavia ran past very near them. Suddenly, with a stamp of feet and a flash of white tails, the two strange rabbits disappeared.

"Come back and play with me!" called the little Rabbit. "Oh, please come back. I KNOW I am Real!"

But there was no answer...only the little ants ran back and forth and the grass swayed gently where the two strange rabbits had passed. The Velveteen Rabbit was all alone.

"Oh," he thought, "why did they run away like that? Why couldn't they stay and talk to me?"

For a long time he stood very still, watching the grass and hoping that they would come back. But they never did...and soon Flavia came and carried him home.

Weeks passed, and the little Rabbit grew very old and shabby, but Flavia loved him just as much. She loved him so much that she loved some of his whiskers off... and the pink lining to his ears had turned pale...and his beautiful coat was now worn and tattered. He even began to lose his shape and to wrinkle, and he scarcely looked like a rabbit any more...except to Flavia. To her he was always beautiful, and that was all that the little Rabbit cared about. He didn't mind how he looked to other people because childhood magic had made him Real...and when you are Real...shabbiness doesn't matter.

And then one day, the Velveteen Rabbit heard the family talking about Flavia. They said she hadn't been feeling well...and now she had a high fever.

Flavia's fever was so high she talked in her sleep, and she was so hot that it almost burned the Rabbit when she held him close. Strange people came and went into the house...and a light burned all night...and the Rabbit could hear Willie crying and he could see that Mama and Mammo and Jack were very worried. All through it, the little Velveteen Rabbit lay there, hidden from sight under the covers...staying close. He never moved when any of them were around, because he was afraid if they found him they might take him away... and he knew that Flavia needed him.

For a long time Flavia was too sick to play, and the little Rabbit found the days empty with nothing to do. He loved her so much that sometimes when he would stand up in bed just to look at her, the love would shine from his eyes.

Then he would snuggle down patiently, and waited for the time when Flavia would be well again . . . and they could go out in the yard among the flowers and under the fig tree . . . and take wagon rides out in the fields behind the house like they used to.

One night, while Flavia lay half asleep, the Rabbit crawled up close to her on the pillow and whispered in her ear all the things they soon would be doing together.

And soon...the fever left and Flavia got better. She was able to sit up in bed and look at picture-books, while the little Rabbit cuddled close at her side. And then finally the day came when she was able to get up and get dressed.

It was a bright morning, and Mammo had opened the windows to let the warm sunshine in. Mama had wrapped Flavia in a quilt, carried her outside and put her in one of the funny old chairs on the porch.

The doctor had told Mama that Flavia needed some fresh air, so they had decided to take her to the ocean the next day. While they were talking and making plans, the little Rabbit lay under the covers, with just his head peeping out, and listened.

"Hooray!" thought the little Rabbit. "Tomorrow we shall go to the beach!" Flavia and Willie had told him about the ocean many times before, and he had wanted very much to see the sea shells, and sand castles and to smell the sea and watch the waves come in.

Just then, Mammo saw him peeping out from under the covers and thought to herself, "I know, I'll throw this shabby old Rabbit away and surprise Flavia with a brand new one when we get to the beach tomorrow."

And so the little Rabbit was gathered up and put into a sack with some other old toys and carried out behind the house to be given away to the Hankyman when he came down the alley next Tuesday.

　　While Flavia was asleep, dreaming of the ocean and the sand castles…the little Rabbit lay among the other old toys beside the back porch…and he felt very lonely. The sack had been left untied, and so by wriggling a bit he was able to get his head through the opening and look out. He was shivering a little, for he had been used to sleeping in a warm bed, and by this time his coat had worn so thin from being hugged that it no longer kept him warm. Nearby, he could see the grass by the edge of the flower bed…it looked very tall and close now, like a tropical jungle, and he watched the shadows fall upon the back porch steps where for so many mornings he and Flavia had played.

Now when he thought of those long sunlit hours in the yard, and how happy he and Flavia had been...a great sadness came over him.

He seemed to see all the times they had had together pass before him, each more beautiful than the next...the afternoons when they would make fairy huts in the flower beds; the times Flavia would talk to him and tie ribbons around his neck; the quiet evenings when they would play in the field and he would watch the little ants run over his paws; and the wonderful day when he first knew that he was Real.

He thought of the Skin Horse, so wise and kind and gentle, and all that he had told him. Then he asked himself, "What good is it to be loved and to lose one's beauty and become Real if it all ends like this?" And a tear, a real tear, trickled down his shabby little velveteen nose and fell to the ground.

And then a strange thing happened...for where the tear had fallen, a flower began to grow out of the ground. A mysterious flower, not at all like any that grew in the yard. It had smooth green leaves the color of emeralds, and in the center of the leaves there was a blossom shaped like a silver cup.

It was so beautiful that the little Rabbit stopped crying...and just lay there watching it.

And then the blossom opened...and out of it there stepped a fairy.

She was the loveliest fairy in the whole world. Her dress was of stardust and dewdrops, and there were flowers around her neck and in her hair.

And she came close to the little Rabbit and gathered him up in her arms and kissed him on his little velveteen nose that was all damp from crying.

"Little Rabbit," she said, "don't you know who I am?"

The Rabbit looked up to her, and it seemed to him that he had seen her face before, but he couldn't think where.

"I am the Childhood Magic Fairy," she said. "I take care of all the special playthings that the children have loved.

When they are old and worn out and none of the children need them anymore, then I come and take them away with me and turn them into Real."

"Wasn't I Real before?" asked the little Rabbit.

"You were Real to Flavia," the Fairy said, "because she loved you. Now you shall be real to everyone."

And she held the little Rabbit close in her arms and flew with him into the field behind the house.

It was lighter now, for the stars were shining. All the night was beautiful, and the dewdrops on the grass shone like frosted silver in the moonlight. In the field the wild rabbits danced with their shadows on the velvet grass, but when they saw the fairy, they all stopped dancing and stood round in a ring to stare at her.

"I've brought you a new friend," the Fairy said. "You must be very kind to him and teach him all he needs to know in Rabbit-land, for he is going to live with you for ever and ever!"

And she kissed the little Rabbit again and put him down on the grass.

"Run and play, little Rabbit!" she said. But the little Rabbit sat quite still for a moment and never moved. For when he saw all the wild rabbits dancing around him, he suddenly remembered about his hind legs and he didn't want them to see that he was made all in one piece. He did not know that when the Fairy kissed him that last time, she had changed him and he was no longer a toy.

He might have sat there a long time, too shy to move, if just then something hadn't tickled his nose . . . and before he thought about what he was doing . . . he lifted his hind toe to scratch it.

He saw that he actually had hind legs! And, instead of old velveteen, he had gray and white fur, soft and shiny . . . and his ears twitched by themselves, and his whiskers were so long that they brushed the grass.

He gave one leap and the joy of using those hind legs was so great that he went dancing about the grass on them, jumping sideways and whirling round the wild flowers as the others did, and he became so excited that when at last he did stop to look for the Fairy, she had gone.

And...he was a REAL rabbit at last!

Autumn passed and Winter, and in the Spring, when the days grew warm and sunny again, Flavia went out to play in the tall grass in the field behind the house.

While she was playing, two rabbits crept out from the grass and peeped at her. One of them was gray all over, but the other had pale markings under his fur, as though a long time ago he might have been winter white.

There was something familiar about his soft nose, and in his eyes there was a look of love. When Flavia moved closer, she saw that when the light shined on his eyes in just a way...they reflected a kind of lavender blue.

At that moment, she knew for certain...this was her old Bunny...come back to look at the child who had loved him, and first helped him to be Real.

Through the years that followed, Flavia and the little Rabbit would think of each other and all that they had learned. During the Summers, Flavia would often leave ribbons at the edge of the field where the tall grass grew...and in the Winters, on the back porch steps. And...always...in the mornings...the ribbons would be gone.

Sometimes the Rabbit would wonder if all that had happened to him with Flavia and the Skin Horse had been a dream, but, like Flavia, he knew that the magic part of being Real meant believing in yourself with all your heart...and knowing you can do whatever you dream you can do.

They had each discovered that it's not always the understanding of life that's really important...but the believing in the wonder of it...and they both knew that when you love someone, REALLY love someone, no matter what, that kind of love never goes away.

THE END